Women who Win Devotionals & Words of Encouragement

Regina Carter

ISBN:-10: 1717292593
ISBN-13: 978-1717292599

DEDICATION

This book is dedicated to Pastor Tommy Carter and the New
Liberty Outreach Church Family!

"Be determined to WIN! If tomorrow is based upon what you do today, how blessed would you be?" Pastor Tommy Carter

God is preparing the way for you. You will not have to fear because the Lord is with you. He is making you the Head and not the tail and what God has for you, is for you. Whatever you put your heart and mind unto shall be yours. What you don't know, the Lord will teach you so don't be afraid to step out on faith and get what God has for you! You must get out of your comfort zone and trust God. It is time to move into what God has in store for you. You will excel as long as you remain in Him.

NOW IS THE TIME!

Pastor Tommy Carter

"For God hath not given us the spirit of fear; but of Power, and of love and of a sound mind." 2 Timothy 1:7

ACKNOWLEDGMENTS

I thank God for choosing me for such a time as this, making, shaping and molding me into what he needed me to be to fulfill his purpose in the earth. I am a living testimony of what God can do in the lives of his people if we just give our lives to him. I'm grateful for my husband and Pastor, Tommy Carter for praying, sharing divine wisdom and encouraging me along the way. I am also thankful for my family and Church family who prayed and inspires me to not only write but continue this walk that the Lord has ordained for me to carry out.

"Two are better than one; because they have a good reward for their labour. For if they fall, the one will lift up his fellow: but woe to him that is alone when he falleth; for he hath not another to help him up." Ecclesiastes 4:9-10

From the Author:

I pray that these simple devotions and words of encouragement motivate and strengthen you in your walk in Christ to become the best that you can be for Him.

WORDS OF ENCOURAGEMENT

Don't quit! There are people you haven't met yet that are counting on you to stay the course!

Never ever give up! Never Quit! Be an Esther, bold and courageous enough to stand for the truth, to voice your opinion, and fight for the good of others even when it means to sacrifice yourself. If God has put you in a position it is for his purpose. Never be afraid to take heed to that inner voice. I encourage you as a woman to delight in what it means to be a woman. Your whole life as a saved woman of excellence will be reviewed and tried by fire. Anything done for self will be burned up and cease to exist. Anything done for God will endure the fire and remain. You will only be rewarded in heaven for what remains. Use your strength on what will remain forever. Use your strength for God! Those who are married use your strength for your husband! For you that are mothers, use your strength for your children! Don't let your strength be misplaced.

"And not only so, but we glory in tribulations also: knowing that tribulation worketh patience; And patience, experience and experience, hope:" Romans 5:3-4

Many a times you find yourself worrying, stressed out, sad or even depressed when various trials come your way but today you must ask yourself, "Where is my Faith?" God says that you should glory in tribulations, not complain. When you glory in your trials you learn patience. You must learn how to trust God to fix your situations. Faith is believing without seeing; allow Faith to have its perfect work in you.

There was a time in my life; while single and raising two kids, that I had to face many trials and I found myself complaining, crying and worrying about how I was going to fix it. I eventually came to the realization that I needed to let God fix it! I soon turned it over to Him and began to just fill my time with working for Him, reading His Word and laying before Him daily seeking His face. Soon the trails worked out and I learned to not only trust Him but wait on Him to fix the situation.

Regardless of what you are facing, God will always make a way. When you are down to nothing, God is always up to something. He is faithful and He is a provider. Put your complete trust in God through every situation believing that He will fix it and give Him the praise in the midst of your trials and watch Him work things out for your good.

Prayer: Father God, forgive me for not putting my full trust in you. Increase my Faith and help me to depend on you regardless of how things may look or even how I may feel. I trust you God with all my heart and my hope is in you. In Jesus Name! Amen.

Inspired by Minister Ashley Fluker

NOTES

Words of Encouragement

Are you more worried about your phone being charged than your spiritual life? Make every effort to put your spiritual life before your phone and social media! Go on a phone fast, a social media fast and you will see how addicted you really are to it. You must become aware of what you are truly hungry for and what you are feeding yourself more of daily! Is it more attention on Facebook, Instagram or other social media outlets or is it God and His Word and prayer? Just something to ponder upon as you draw closer to God and separate yourself from the world!

Prayer: Lord allow me to be hungrier for you, your Word, and your Will instead of the world and all it has to offer! Let me utilize these social media outlets to glorify you and show less of me! Help me to stop seeking the attention of the world and seek to obtain your attention as I obtain a closer walk with you! I have nothing to prove to the world besides that you are the one true God and the only way out! It is not about me but about the work you have purposed for me to do! In Jesus Name! Amen

"But seek ye first the kingdom of God, and his righteousness; and all these things shall be added unto you." Matthew 6:33

Many times, when you are going through, you seek everything else first before seeking God. You find yourself asking others' opinions, making your own decisions, or assumptions, stressing, getting depressed or even just giving up and throwing in the towel. But God is saying "SEEK ME"- Seek my Kingdom- Seek my Righteousness- FIRST! Not after you have tried everything else, and then everything else will be added unto you. That is a promise from God so seek and you will find everything you so desire or need in Him alone.

Take some time today to write down everything that you are praying for the Lord to do in your life. Set aside a place in your home in a closet or in a corner or in an empty room where you pray if you haven't done so. Hang up your petitions on the wall and as the Lord answer your prayers, right the date beside each petition and keep it there as a witness to what God has already done for you. When you get in a place to where you are doubting just go back to your prayer wall and remember what God has already done. Know that if He did it before, He surely will do it again.

Prayer: Father God forgive me for not seeking you first in all that I do, Today is a new day that I am deciding to seek you, your kingdom and your righteousness first and I know that everything else will be added in Jesus Name!

NOTES

WORDS OF ENCOURAGEMENT!

"It's not about the destination you are trying to reach but about the journey to get there" Pastor Tommy Carter

Be watchful, prayerful and sensitive to the voice of the Lord! You never know whose waiting on the side of the road that you are assigned to deliver. We must be about our Father's business because souls are waiting for us! Remember, only what you do for Christ will last! There is no fear in love! Perfect love casteth out fear! I pray that you seek God's perfect love in others and not put up walls of fear with those whom God has allowed His love to fill and give unto you. My prayer is that you discern between God's love and the lust and deception of the world. May the grace of God be upon you and His perfect Will be manifested in you. It is time to prepare yourself and make room for what the Lord has spoken in your life! Wake up Expecting, Worshipping God, and Believing and watch Him bring it to pass! All you need is one touch from the Lord! Don't you dare get weary in well doing, because in due season you will reap if you faint not. Remember that you are a person of influence and you are influencing people daily! Now go and be the difference maker! Those days that you are literally living off the prayers of the righteous makes you grateful for those that really touch God on your behalf!

"…. neither be ye sorry; for the joy of the Lord is your strength." Nehemiah 8:10

Many a times in life you have experienced or may even be experiencing right now, challenge after challenge but if you maintain your Joy in the Lord, He will become your strength.

Going through a divorce with children was a great challenge for me. Through this trial I experienced fear because I didn't know what to expect being a single parent. I worked full-time, attended College and just had experienced a bankruptcy. Through it all, I had to step out on faith and trust God. Some days were better than others and the enemy tried to fight time after time in my mind but through prayer and reading God's Word, I gained strength and the encouragement to not give up. Today I can testify that I made it through!

Regardless of what you may be experiencing or how the enemy may fight, be encouraged, stand on God's Word and never give up. Stay focused on God's plan for your life and the joy of the Lord will be your strength.

Prayer: Lord I thank you for encouraging me on today. The enemy cannot have my joy. You are my strength Lord when I am weak. Allow me to keep my eyes focused on you and your Word in times of weakness and maintain my joy in Jesus Name! Amen

Inspired by Carolyn Goosby

NOTES

WORDS OF ENCOURAGEMENT!

Be stronger than you excuse! Be intentional about utilizing your gifts to make your ministry better in whatever capacity that you can maintain. Pray about being a better servant to help grow the ministry that the Lord has placed you in giving it your all. Be intentional about seeing your ministry grow and move forward, remembering that this is not just about you but about the work that God has in store for you to fulfill. Begin to put in your heart the things that you would like to offer your ministry and stop expecting others to do all of the work while you wait on blessings! Stop looking for the perfect church and you be a better church member by being an example of the true church to others. Make God your priority! Pray for spiritual growth, an increase in your giving, and a mind to want to be a part of bringing your ministry's vision to pass. Sow in faith and sow your way out of poverty, sickness, weaknesses, and trials believing God will do and watch him move on your behalf!

The Lord is my Shepherd; I shall not want. Psalm 23:1

When we look at a Shepherd, we see that it's their duty to tend to, guide, and direct in a particular direction. There may be times that you feel like you are alone in this walk with God. When the pressures of life get to you and you feel like all is lost you can look unto the hills from whence cometh your help! The Lord will lead and guide you as your shepherd and if you trust Him, you shall not want. He will be your provider, your protector and your supplier of all your needs. When your back is against the wall and there seems to be nowhere to turn look up and say

"Lord you are my shepherd, I shall not want."

Reflection: Is there anything too hard for God? NO! Trust Him to lead and guide you in the right direction and you will never fail.

Inspired by Shelia Goosby

NOTES

WORDS OF ENCOURAGEMENT!

Just to be able to hear from God and allow Him to show us things mightily while revealing His Word to us is indeed a blessing alone. The strength to go on when others are giving up so easily! Having the Faith to stand even in trials! Experiencing true deliverance! Having access to the Father! Our names being written! Our life, health, and strength! Divine protection! A mind to want to serve Him in spite of! My God! I can go on and on, we have so much to be thankful for! The Bible says that many shall fall away from the Faith running after what they want to hear and not the truth that would bring forth their deliverance, men will take silly women captive seducing them and drawing them right into the devil's trap! But we shall stand! Don't you dare let nothing separate you, It's not even worth it! I would rather struggle here in Jesus than to go back to a world that I know will spend eternity in hell! So, I encourage you to keep humbling yourself, keep praying and seeking the Lords face and Turn from your wicked ways and He will hear you, heal you and forgive you!

For I reckon that the suffering of this present time are not worthy to be compared with the glory which shall be revealed in us. Romans 8:18

You may be feeling the pressure right now. You may be at the end of your rope. You may want to throw in the towel. You may be feeling as if you are hanging on by a thread. You don't see a way out. You're feeling overwhelmed, stressed, and even though you know what God has promised and what He can do, the weight of all the pressure is on your shoulders weighing you down. RISE UP! You can do this! He will do it in you because He is your strength when you are weak. The struggle may be real, But God is greater, the finances may be low, But God is a provider. Your body may be racking with pain, But God is a healer. So, get up and look in the mirror and say: "I am a Winner!" Get up and put a praise on your lips telling God THANK YOU in advance. Keep looking up unto the hills from whence cometh your help and tell God "I thank you that you have already heard me!" Now wait on the promise and go in peace! Every time the enemy places a negative thought in your mind cast it down and speak life, speak God's Word, speak God's promises over your life and your God shall supply all of your needs according to His riches in glory.

Reflection: Reflect back on what God has already done for you in the past and know that if He did it before, He can do it again! Be encouraged!

NOTES

PRAYER

Father, with my eyes lifted towards heaven, I call on you right now! You know my needs, my struggles, my desires when I'm weak and when I'm strong. According to thy Word you said that I could call on your name and you would answer. I need you to strengthen me for the journey, equip me in the spirit of my mind to stand strong in adversity and heal my body so that I can be an effective witness for you. You created me for good works. Whatever is holding me back from good works, remove it so that I can perform those things you have created me to do and so that others may see your glory in me. I thank you father that you love me regardless of where I am or where I have been in life. I praise you now for being my source and strength. You are the everlasting God, our Prince of peace, the one and only true God, the true source of all we can imagine or even think. You are God alone! By thy name Jesus I pray, Amen!

Inspired by Tommy Carter

Thy mercy is in the heavens and thy faithfulness reacheth into the clouds. Psalm 36:5

You may be feeling like you can't do enough for God or be good enough for Him, but God's mercy and faithfulness is not based upon what one may do or say. His love never fails, nor does it ever change. Put your full trust in Him, believing that He will take care of you. You are made righteous through the precious blood of Jesus and not through your own righteousness. Be encouraged! You are not perfect, but you can be obedient to God's Word and He shall supply all your needs according to His riches in glory. Don't beat yourself up so much. You may fall from time to time but get back up, repent and start over because the Lord truly knows your heart and His faithfulness and mercy are new every morning.

Prayer: Lord help me to understand that my works and righteousness is not what make you love me more but it's only by the blood of Jesus that I am made righteous. Help me to remain faithful and obedient to your Word and Will for my life and understand that you love me past my faults, in Jesus Name, Amen.

Inspired by Ursala McCarty

NOTES

WORDS OF ENCOURAGEMENT!

Every time I rise, my mouth opens daily tell God to "CHANGE ME!" CHANGE ME OH GOD surrounds me in my office to remind me that it's about ME having that right relationship with God regardless of what others do or say. You be the example! You be the light! You be the witness! How are others going to come out if you act like they act or do the things that they do or even say the things that they say? You can make the difference in others' lives. Don't allow the enemy to taint your witness, keep your character and your integrity wherever you may be and regardless of what may happen. Stop blaming others for the way you're acting because that gives them power over you. Control your own emotions, thoughts and attitude in every situation, it can be done because God's spirit is within you! Rise up and be the best YOU that you can be! Regardless how far you think you are still utter the words "CHANGE ME OF GOD!"

I dare you to touch God! I mean really get up from whatever has been holding you back and touch Him. Yes! He will make you whole again, He will give life to a dead situation, He will loose the shackles, He will break the yokes that are keeping you bound, so get up! Yield yourself to Him completely and He will bring you out victoriously. After all that I have been through, all that I have experienced, all of the blessings and the prayers I have seen brought to pass and even all of the doors that I have seen shut on my behalf; my prayer is still "CHANGE ME OH GOD, make me more like you, wash me through and through, create in me a clean heart so that I may worship you." I encourage you today to humble yourself under the mighty hand of God, remain obedient, continue to pray that His Will be done and not your own and the Lord will exalt you in due season.

Psalm 85:8 says, "I will HEAR what GOD the LORD will speak: for He will speak unto His people, and to His Saints: but let them not turn again to folly." Once the Lord speaks, we should HEAR, OBEY, and DO what His Word says and never leave out the same! You have the POWER to make the difference, be the example and be the change that you want to see!

Thy Word is a lamp unto my feet, and a light unto my path.
Psalm 119:105

Today I feel like John crying out in the wilderness saying "Repent, repent for the kingdom of heaven is at hand!" I feel like shouting out "Jesus!" My God, it's just in my spirit; I feel like running on to see what the end is going to be. Stir up the gift that's within you! Refuse to face another day dealing with circumstances the same way that you always have. Be the difference maker in your own life and stop waiting on others to make a difference. God's power is within you and He alone will be a lamp unto your feet and a light unto your path. Rise up and conquer! You can do it! With God all things are possible only if you believe.

Prayer: God, today I just want to say Thank you for being God all by yourself. You are truly all that I need, and I will be more than a conqueror from this day forward. I put my full trust in you and believe that you will lead and direct my path. In Jesus name! Amen!

NOTES

WORDS OF ENCOURAGEMENT!

Lord have mercy! I made It and got a message in the process! I decided to start riding my bike today and not wait until tomorrow on my journey to a better me. As I begin to ride down my street it was easy, and I was smiling saying "I got this!" Of course, I was going down the hill, so I didn't have to do nothing but ride till I got around the curve and started going up. The ride was getting harder and harder because of the resistance and lack of exercise on my part but I still kept pumping. As I made it to the next street and looked up, the hill was even steeper, but I begin to pump anyway until I couldn't pump no more. I decided to stop and rest and try again two or three times then I had a thought to just turn around and go back the way that I came because it looked to hard but I rebuked that negativity and decided to push my bike and just walk up the hill. By the time I made it half way up the hill I decided to get back on and try again and I made it to the top because of determination even though it hurt and I was cold because of the wintery weather, I still pushed myself to complete the task praying of course the entire time. When I saw my house, my strength came, and I was really moving giving it all I got because I saw the end coming and I made it. I said that to say this, throughout our journey in our spiritual lives we will experience some good easy times as well as some hard rough times but we must keep the faith and keep pressing toward the mark not allowing obstacles to stop us nor turn us around. Sometimes we may have to stop and just rest then move forward than at other times we may have to push our way when we have resistance from the enemy allowing the Lord to give us the strength to keep moving forward. In the end we will see that no matter how we finished whether walking, running, crawling or holding on by a thread we still will win. This race isn't given to the swift, neither to the strong but to the one that endures until the end. Keep praying, pressing, and striving YOU WILL WIN. Pray for endurance and patience throughout your journey.

Oh, Praise the Lord all ye Nations, praise Him all ye people"
Psalm 117:1

Let everything that has breath praise the Lord! The enemy wants you to complain, stress, worry and walk in unbelief and doubt when you experience situations, but I dare you to praise God even in the midst of your storms! When you are feeling down- Praise Him! When you are broke (in between blessings) and bills are due- Praise Him! If you lose your job- Praise Him! When you are sick- Praise Him! When you are all alone- Praise Him and watch God turn things around for you. The Lord inhabits the praises of His people and when praises go up, we know that blessings will come down. Don't allow the enemy to win, praise God in the midst of any and every situation and He will see you through.

Prayer: Lord I thank you for a heart filled with praise! With you in my life, all things are possible only if I believe. I will continue to give you all of the praise, the honor, and the glory forever and ever. In Jesus Name! Amen!

Inspired by Teona Williams

NOTES

WORDS OF ENCOURAGEMENT

This is the day that the Lord has made, you should rejoice and be glad in it! It is time for you to return to your first love! Get back to the feet of Jesus and stay locked in! This is not the time to be in and out, but it is the time to DECIDE who you really choose to serve. Stay grounded and rooted in God and let nothing move you. Stay faithful and committed no matter what it costs you! The tree is being shaken but you must hold on! Pull down strongholds, you have the power to do so! Don't be moved by what you see or hear, the enemy will do anything to get you out of your place so watch with your spiritual eyes and ears open! With God, you are promised the victory, keep standing and building yourself up on your most holy faith. Draw closer and closer to God while you maintain a right relationship with him. Continue to be the light and a source of God's power and peace. Adorn yourself in prayer as things wax worse and worse upon the earth and God will cover you. You may experience terrible effects, but you will not be defeated! Victory belongs to you!

Beloved, think it not strange concerning the fiery trial which is to try you, as though some strange thing happened unto you: but rejoice, in as much as ye are partakers of Christ's sufferings; that when His glory shall be revealed, ye may be glad also with exceeding joy. I Peter 4:12-13

As I sat in church expecting a mighty Word from God, as always, the Lord moved through the Man of God and He spoke that God's grace would be upon each of us. The Word was to present our bodies as a living sacrifice and not to conform to this world but renew our minds. Though my soul did burn, immediately after service I received a call that revealed that someone was spreading lies against me and trying to divide my sisters and myself. I found myself feeling down in my spirit because of the source that I knew that this came from, but I had to remember who I am and whose I am and gave it to God in prayer. I begin to count it all joy knowing when truth is spoken deception would always be revealed and God gave me peace along with the will to pray for their deliverance. Regardless of what you may be facing, think it not strange! Don't lose your focus, keep presenting your body as a living sacrifice unto God even if you have to do it alone. You don't have to prove yourself to no one, only prove what is that good and acceptable and perfect will of God. Renew your mind and maintain God's purpose in you and let Him take care of your enemies for you. This should only give you the strength to pour yourself more in the will of God knowing that it is only by Him that we live, move and have our being.

Prayer: God, I thank you now for being my protector and my keeper. You said in your Word that vengeance belongs to you and you would prepare a table before me in the presence of my enemies. Help me to keep my eyes on you and your will for me. In Jesus name! Amen!

NOTES

WORDS OF ENCOURAGEMENT

Go out and be the light! You are the light of the world! Walk in your God given purpose and remember to prepare for the promise God has given you. Stop going around the same mountain over and over again. Rise above yourself and seek the kingdom! Draw nigh unto God and he will draw nigh unto you! Stop running, hiding and making excuses and come to the light! Don't you dare sit back and let the devil keep you in a snare from your purpose. There is not one excuse that should keep you from the presence of God. Choose ye this day who you will serve! If you are not putting God first and being obedient to his Will, whatever you are doing will never work! It will be good for a little while, but you will stumble, you will reach rock bottom, and the only thing that can bring you out is God. Please trust Him and rise above where you are by serving him, doing his Will, and allowing him to do the rest. Every good and perfect gift comes from above. Stop letting the devil make you believe that you are being blessed by God and be comfortable with staying where you are. Bind the devil, submit yourself to God, resist him and he has to flee.

My Grace is sufficient for thee, for my strength is made perfect in weakness: most gladly therefore, will I rather glory in my infirmities that the Power of Christ may rest upon me. II Corinthians 12:9

Today was a day that came with much pressure! I was overwhelmed with each trial that came my way and right when I felt like I was about to break, I grabbed my purse and my keys and just took a break. Once I made it to my car, I called my husband and spoke with him about the matter and being the Man of God that he is, of course he said that everything would be okay. After getting off the phone I could feel a tear about to drop but suddenly the Holyghost rose up in me and I said "Lord your grace is sufficient for me, when the enemy comes in like a flood, I know that you will raise up a standard against him; so Lord I trust you!" Immediately I felt strength to go on and suddenly my phone went off and it

was the Pastor of the church we had recently been blessed with letting me know that he had good news for me and that we could move into our new church building two weeks earlier than expected. All I could say is "Lord thank you for always showing up right on time, reminding me that you are a very present help in the times of trouble."

Be encouraged on today! Keep trusting God with all your heart and lean not unto your own understanding! Right when your blessing is about to come, the enemy will always try and cause some commotion to go on to make you lose focus but stand your ground and seek the Lord even the more. There is a blessing in the pressing and the Lord won't put no more on you than you can bear. Better days are coming!

Prayer: Lord, I thank you for showing yourself strong over and over again in my life. Thank you for supplying all of my needs according to your riches in glory. Help me to continue to put all my trust in you regardless of the situations that are going on around me. In Jesus name! Amen!

Inspired by Evangelist Richena Richmond

NOTES

WORDS OF ENCOURAGEMENT

While sitting here reflecting back on past decisions that I made in my life, I realized that the Lord has been showing us things all along and we just fail to see them for what they are. When the Lord put things together, we got to learn to appreciate it and know that it is for His purpose and not just for this flesh or to fulfill our own lustful desires that we need deliverance from. So many times we allow our flesh to dictate who we are and what we should be or do and not be spiritually minded which blinds us from seeing the enemy trying to slowly pull apart what God has put together for His purpose and not our own. He then turns around and show you the people you were looking at in the flesh spiritually and we are blinded by the flesh so we can't see it. We must start seeing things through the eyes of the Christ and from his perspective in order to truly be free. It is the enemies desire to sift of as wheat a little at a time! This is often a slow process like cheating where it starts out by looking upon someone with lustful eyes, then you find yourself in a place to where you cannot wait to see them, then it moves to secret text, phone calls, and conversations, then the physical part begins. Do you ever notice when the enemy has his hands in things it's done secretly, or you have to hide to do them? So, if you are in any situation that you have to sneak and hide to accomplish it, I encourage you to RUN for your life, it's a TRAP! We must watch, fight, and pray for discernment.

Fear thou not; for I am with thee: be not dismayed, for I am thy God: I will strengthen thee; yea, I will help thee; yea, I will uphold thee with the right hand of my righteousness. Isaiah 41:10.

God says " I will help thee" I always hear people say "I'm waiting on God" well, God is not going to do it all for you, He says that He will help you- meaning that He will assist you in doing whatever it is that you are desiring to do but you must take the first step in Faith and do the work. While you are waiting on God, sometimes He is just waiting on you to move. He will help lead and guide you in the right direction. It is time to stop complaining and murmuring and start moving in Faith. You must know who you are in Christ- Know your identity. If you don't know who you are you will always become whatever other people think you should be and never be your true self. If you knew who you were you would believe that you can do all things and have confidence in yourself. Change your mindset!

If you don't like your job- pray and go fill out applications for another.

If you want to go to college- apply and do the necessary steps to get admitted.

If you want that house- get your credit together and search for homes.

If you want a Godly husband/wife- learn how to be a Godly husband/wife.

If you want a car- save for a down payment or pay it off in full.

Most of all- learn how to draw closer to God, read His Word, pray daily, fast, learn of His love and then you will know how to recognize real love from others. Ask God for His divine wisdom, knowledge, and understanding while learning to hear His voice. Knowledge is Power! Know that the greatest resistance comes when you are positioned near the greatest opportunity!

Stop trying to manage something that you can't fix!

Stop putting too much energy into things that are not profitable!

Make every step count!

Get tired of going through circles in the wilderness!

Stop focusing on what is around you and focus on God! Faith moves and pleases God! Get in position for your blessings, get organized, get your house in order and you will reap what you sow.

Inspired by Alicia Thomas

NOTES

WORDS OF ENCOURAGEMENT:

How bad do you want it?
How bad do you want His favor?
How bad do you want His Love?
How bad do you want His blessings?
How bad do you want the Anointing?
How bad do you want to be Victorious?
How bad do you want Eternal Life?
How bad do you want your Deliverance?
How bad do you want Healing?

What will you sacrifice to get it and keep it?
What will you give up?
How bad do you really want it?

Just something to think about and consider on this week. God is looking for Laborers, true soldiers! He is trying to equip you for battle, but you must get in place to be equipped then you won't fall... He said that He will give His Angels charge over you to keep you in ALL our ways...

Are you allowing the Angels and God to keep you?
Or are you letting flesh, pride, pity, overtake you?
Remain prayerful and have a quiet spirit so that the Lord can give you direction. You must BE STILL so you can hear. Do not be a busy body especially if it's keeping you out of the presence of God and out of your rightful place.
You are Victorious!
You are a Triumphant Warrior!
You have Power!
Use it!

Let the redeemed of the Lord say so! Who He hath redeemed from the hand of the enemy. Psalm 107:2.

I was talking to the Lord about a situation that kind of bothered me and He reminded me of this scripture, and I had to share it! Saints as we are fighting this good fight of faith some things should be expected. We should not even be surprised at the enemy tactics nor let them bother us because we have Power over the enemy, so as I sit here thinking about some things that is vexing my spirit, the Lord said "SO!"

When people are lying on you- say SO!

When people misuse you- say SO!

When people talk about you- say SO!

When trials and tribulations come- say SO!

We are redeemed by the blood of the lamb, which is Jesus Christ, so if God didn't say it, then it shouldn't bother us. He is the ultimate judge of the intent of people hearts so don't sit up and miss God or your blessings because of what someone else has said or did, it only gives the enemy power over you. Today I can stand and say, "SO devil, I've already been redeemed from your hand, so I resist you and you will have to flee." Yes! I still have my Joy! I still have my peace! I still have love for the brethren! I declare and decree it in Jesus name and ask God to forgive them that know not what they do. This is my testimony and I am sticking to it! I can stand and testify today so others can overcome! Don't allow the enemy to get your focus off of what the Lord is trying to do for you and in you! As long as the Lord knows, it doesn't matter what others may think or say, God will always expose the enemy to those that are His so just pray for them and keep fighting for your blessings. God says that He would prepare a table before you right in the presence of your enemies and they will know that God is with you. Be encouraged: God is not through with you yet, I don't care if you messed up today; Repent and get back up, the Lord has his hands extended waiting to put you right back in your rightful place.

NOTES

WORDS OF ENCOURAGEMENT!

Years ago, Pastor Carter spoke Hebrews 10:36 to me when I was in a moment of impatience, which says: "You are in need of patience, after you have done the Will of God, you shall receive the promise." The more I read this scripture, the more nuggets drop in my spirit. God wants us to be faithful to his Word, statutes, as servants and so forth. He rewards faithfulness and this is why we are in need of patience, in order to endure hardship like a good soldier and not give up or give in to the enemy's tactics. Even if you are hanging on by a thread, you keep going by Faith, hearing the Word so that the Lord can give you more strength to change and become more like him. The more you surround yourself with him, the better you will become! The more you surround yourself with the things that are no like him the farther away you will become! You got to keep pressing! The longer you fight against and run from correction or truth, the longer you stay where you are. Come out from among them and be separate saith the Lord! God is bidding us to come to him! You can't fix things on your own, it takes action, so you have to move and do something about it!

"But Jesus beheld them, and said unto them, With men this is impossible; but with God all things are possible." Matthew 19:26

I woke up this morning singing "I will bless the oh Lord!" The Lord will set things in order for you now that He has set you free. He will set your feet on a firm foundation and set you on fire for His glory. What He sets in place and establish by His name no one can move nor can they undo it. But you must turn your heart toward Him, and He will turn to you. God will establish you in His love and remove all of your shame. Set your heart on Him and He will bless you- Set your mind on Him and on things above and He will show you great and mighty things that you have never known. Yes! He will open up His hidden mysteries to you. There is nothing too hard for God- no problem is to challenging for Him. He wants to deliver you and place you in His perfect Will. He will bring you out and draw you closer to Him. Many times, you are waiting on God, but He is waiting on you! He desires you praise- He desires for you to talk to Him in Faith believing that what you ask Him for will be done in Jesus name. He has destiny waiting for you- He has purpose for you- You will be transformed in your mind, your heart, even in your walk! He will change you; He will bless you- but you must allow Him to set things in order for you.

Today, give God all you got! Walk in truth, walk in integrity, and keep a good character. You are God's extremities in the earth so show forth His goodness, His love, His compassion, His Joy, His Peace, His Patience, Self-control, and His Meekness in all that you do from this day forward! When God is ordering your steps sin will not dominate you no longer and fear will no longer run your life. So, Rise up with Fire in your hands, Fire in your feet, and Fire in your mouth! YOU HAVE POWER! For He whom the Son sets free is free indeed!

NOTES

WORDS OF ENCOURAGEMENT!

Be grateful for the people God has placed in your life that love you enough to see you succeed and not just stay where you are! God love you enough to send the right people at the right time to lead you in the right direction, but you got to see it and accept it in order to move forward. Take inventory on your life to see if you are moving forward in Jesus, going backwards or still the same. You must choose the direction you want your life to go in and take action. You must choose where you want to spend eternity and take action. This is a heart condition and wherever your treasure is, meaning whatever you love the most, this is where your heart will be. Start making decisions based upon the Word of God and not your flesh. God wants to save and deliver you so don't be found as the five foolish virgins letting your oil run out and expecting the five wise virgins to lend them some of theirs. You got to get this on your own!

Have not I commanded thee? Be strong and of a good courage; be not afraid, neither be thou dismayed: for the Lord thy God is with thee withersoever thou goest. Joshua 1:9

It's only a season for what you are going through but stay focused and never lose sight. I know others may not see or even understand the hurt you are feeling inside but keep on smiling knowing that everything will be alright. You got to believe that better days are coming. Living for God is not hard, it's the dying daily to this flesh that seems to hold you back. Even in the darkest of times, know that God is with you, you are not alone! This is where true faith kicks in. Is there anything too hard for God? He is a way maker, promise keeper, deliverer, life giver, a light in the darkest of place and a miracle worker. Trust Him! Cast down every imagination that tries to exalt itself above the knowledge of God and bring into captivity every thought under the obedience of Christ continuously submitting yourself to Him, resisting the devil and he must flee. You must experience the Word in order to express it, so tough times will come, struggles will come, trials will come, but keep holding on to the Word of God and humble yourself in the sight of God and in due season he will exalt you. The Word is alive, but you just got to see it through the eyes of the Lord. Remain God conscious and aware that the Lord is not just with you, but he is in you and that is where the blessings will lie. You are more than a conqueror only if you believe.

Prayer: Thank you Jesus for being my way of escape in any situation or circumstance that I may be going through. Help me to be strong and courageous knowing that you are with me wherever I may go. I will no longer be afraid for you have not giving me a spirit of fear but of Power, love and a sound mind. I humbly submit myself to you and will continue to die daily. In Jesus name! Amen.

Inspired by Robbin Cook

NOTES

WORDS OF ENCOURAGEMENT

You must remain in Him. You never know whose depending on you! Who are you encouraging? Who are you helping to hold on? Whose changing because of you? Be the best YOU that YOU can be every day. You can't give up nor give in, someone else's lie depends upon it. Failure is not an option; excuses is no longer an option. You have come to far to turn around to dead things again. Be aware that others are observing you and admiring you. You have an influence on others. It is the spirit within you that does the drawing of other to Christ. You must not walk in the flesh but in the spirit so that others may see the Christ in you which is the hope of glory. I encourage you to keep moving forward and continue to walk in your true deliverance. If you really knew the battle that you were really fighting in and what you are really fighting against, you would not take your life in God for granted. You would not be unstable; you would not be in one day and out the next. This is an urgent cry for you to get yourself together before it is too late. Stop taking the Lord's grace in vain. Keep pressing toward the mark and remain in him as the example that others need for their true deliverance. Be the influence and change that you want to see. That the Lord for his mercy toward you, for choosing you, and not rejecting you. Thank him for calling you out and giving you true victory over the enemy, for using you for his glory. Now it is time to walk in what God has ordained in you. You are past excuses at this point, and it is time to move on to save a generation. Give God glory for what he has done on this day alone just for you.

Let us therefore come boldly unto the throne of grace, that we may obtain mercy, and find grace to help in time of need. Hebrews 4:16

I may not know you, but I am sitting here excited about the potential that God has in you and how far you have come. My soul is filled with Joy knowing that you are growing by leaps and bounds, allowing faith to be spoken out of your mouth and walking in it. The Lord is doing such great thing in you and he is moving upon you. Keep moving forward regardless of where you are knowing that his grace is still sufficient for you. He has purpose for you- He has a plan for you- all you have to do is believe it, receive it and walk in it. He has promises waiting just for you, but you must get up and grab them by faith while walking in his Word with obedience. Separate yourself from the world and follow after his Word. He chose you for such a time as this- all you have to do is change your mindset, identify who you really are in him, take on his mind and not your own thinking, walk in his promises and his Word continuously dying to yourself daily, and becoming more like him.

Your old way of living only brought forth temporary fixes, lies, manipulation, deception, broken promises and death. Jesus is the ONLY way out- Doing it his way is the ONLY true way. So, rise up! Don't you dare sell yourself short of God's glory and plans that he has just for you with temporary setbacks that keep you in a state of sin, that keeps you in the devil's trap. Break yourself loose and be all that God has predestined you to be as a Son of God so others can see his good works in you and glorify your God. Go boldly to the throne of grace telling the Lord about your troubles, about your shortcomings, about your weaknesses and let him fix it, let his grace and mercy help you in the times of need.

Prayer: Thank you Lord that I know that I can come to you in prayer in my times of need to obtain your grace and your mercy. Help me to identify who you are and who I am in you to overcome obstacles that may come. Thank you for being a God of another chance and loving me enough to show me myself in order to become what you have already preordained me to be. In Jesus Name! Amen.

Inspired by Valarie Clayton

NOTES

"My brethren, count it all joy when ye fall into divers temptations; knowing this, that the trying of your Faith worketh patience." James 1:23

Today while eating dinner out TV went out while my husband was hooking up a cord to it- But God! I spent four hours on my homework and after entering it all into the computer, almost to the very end the computer blanked out- But God! I stopped, took a deep breath and just closed the computer and whispered "Lord, I Thank You." I went to take a shower and while in there I begin to pray a simple prayer of thanks to the Lord then I got out and went into my prayer room just to spend some alone time with God and reflect back on my day. I was reminded that after all that I had experienced just today alone- I still had my Joy- my Peace- and was able to control my emotions in the midst of it all. I realized that I could use these very trials to encourage someone else.

Today you may be experiencing some trials or tribulations that may seem like they are getting the best of you but remember God's grace is sufficient for you! He will take what the devil meant for bad and turn it around for your good. Don't fret or lose your mind but continue to press in spite of how you may feel. You have the Power to create an atmosphere of Joy and Peace in the midst of any situation. Just stop what you are doing and take a Prayer break and begin to thank God for who He is and what He has done for you and count it all JOY!

Prayer: Lord, thank you for every trial and circumstance that I may be facing on today alone. My joy still remains, and my patience is increase knowing that all things are working together for my good because I love you and I am call according to your purpose. This too shall pass, and you will never put no more on me than I can bear so I will continue to press toward the mark of the high calling which is in Christ Jesus. Thank you for joy and peace in the midst of the storm. In Jesus name. Amen!

Inspired by: Rochelle Wilson

NOTES

WORDS OF ENCOURAGEMENT!

It is not just about YOU when it comes to God's purpose! Stop trying to put yourself first and other things before your precious time with God! Sometimes we wonder why things are not going right and it is because we are putting everything else before him and giving him the leftovers. Matthew 6:33 says "Seek ye first the kingdom of God and his righteousness then all these other things will be added unto you." As long as you are putting everything else first it will never work! Whatever you are putting before him becomes your God so take some time out to think about what you are choosing as your God! Will it be material things, relationships, your job, your money, your family, your children, or sin? You Decide! The Lord is calling for us to come unto him, we must heed the warning and not wait until something happen or let it be too late. So many people are dying outside the Will of God and will not enter into the Kingdom.

We must open our eyes and see the true intent of the enemy, he doesn't care about you, he just wants you to join him in hell. It is his will for you to keep making excuses, keep yourself away from the light outside the Will of God for your life, stuck in your addictions, habits, and weaknesses. He keeps it good enough for you to crave it more and more and every time you try to come out something else happens to make you run right back to it. When you finally realize that it's really not working, that it's really holding you back and keeping you in the wilderness like the Israelites were for forty years, you will finally realize that you need to change because it is not working.

Have you ever been in a place where you have smoked, drank, laid up, worked lots of hours, helped everyone else, put all of your joy and strength into everything else and yet still feel a void? Do you still feel empty? Do you still feel lost? Do you still feel depressed, angry, and unhappy? Do you still experience pain, have no hope or in a moment of despair? God is saying "Come unto me, all ye that are heavy laden, and I will give you rest. Take my yoke upon you and learn of me; for I am meek and lowly in heart: and ye shall find rest unto your soul." He's waiting to fill you with living water and once he fills you, you will never thirst for unrighteousness again unless you choose to. Come to Jesus now! He never fails! You have a promise, you have potential, and you have purpose! Jesus is the only way out!

And that they may recover themselves out of the snare of the devil, who are taken captive by him at his will. II Timothy 2:26

Come out of the trap the enemy has you in, you have power to do so. Don't you dare let him win any longer! He will keep you at home laying down, but God says to STAND! Even in the midst of your struggles, keep pressing forward toward the mark of the high calling. Keep going to the house of God to hear the Word that will be able to lead you and guide you in the right direction. Your deliverance is in and through the Word, that is why the enemy works so hard to keep you from hearing it, because he knows if you feed your mind the Word long enough, it will set you free. If you are constantly surrounded by the saints long enough, you will figure out who you really are and come all the way out. So, you must see where you are right now by taking a look through the eyes of Christ. Are you really allowing God to lead you or the devil? Are you really putting God first in everything that you do, or do you just give him time when you feel like it? Do you put work, kids, relationships and other things before him? Are you spending quality time with him or more time with the devil doing things outside the Will of God? Are you obedient? Are you sacrificing your own desires for his? You must see it and change your mindset, loose insecurities and the lies that the devil has led you to believe and rise up. It first comes with a desire to do so though. If you really want to live you will come out. All the way out and serve God wholeheartedly. If not, you will continue to be double minded and unstable in all of your ways and die, spending eternity with your father the devil. The choice is yours! Meditate on this and decide to LIVE!

Reflection: Take some time out to write some things down that you are still dealing with and areas that you need God's deliverance in. Take a day out of each week to fast and pray to the Lord on these things seeking your deliverance and a better relationship with Him! As you decrease, he will increase in you!

NOTES

WORDS OF ENCOURAGEMENT

When I look at you as a Woman of Excellence,

I don't see failures, shortcomings or struggles.

Faults, weaknesses, or mistakes.

Strongholds, fear or insecurities.

I see purpose, victory and breakthrough.

Deliverance, perfection and confidence.

Virtue, potential, and faithfulness.

Love, joy and peace.

Commitment, blessings, and an example.

True love is patient, love is kind.

It does not envy, it does not boast, it is not proud.

It does not dishonor others, it is not self-seeking, it is not easily angered.

It keeps no record of wrongs. Love does not delight in evil but rejoices in truth.

It always protects, always trusts, always hopes, always perseveres.

True love never fails.

Ye are of God, little children, and have over them: because greater is he that is in you, than he that is in the world. I John 4:4

When you talk about having strength, you are generally referring to being physically or mentally strong. However, there is a strength that reaches beyond human capability- beyond what your body or mind could produce. That is the strength that Jesus promises to all believers. When you know God, you will be made strong because "as He is, so are we in the world". John gives us a greater confidence by declaring that the One inside us is greater than the one who is in this present and evil world. This implies that, because of the power of the Son of God living inside of us, this strength and power is greater than our enemy's power and strength. Therefore, we have the capacity to display his brightness and brilliance in this treasure that is in earthen vessels, that the excellency of power may be of God and not of us. When we are put on display, it is not us, but his glory that is being revealed, this is why James tells us to have joy in tribulations because it is in our weaknesses that Jesus', the source of all power be lifted up. He must increase but we muse decrease.

Prayer: Lord I thank you for choosing me as your own. Help me to realize that it is you who is greater within me than what I may face within this world. I trust you with all of my being and know that when I am weak, that is when you become strong within me. Amen.

NOTES

WORDS OF ENCOURAGEMENT

Are you truly being all that you can be for God? If not, why? What's holding you back from totally surrendering to God's Will knowing that his Will is the only perfect plan for your life that has long lasting results. Don't you dare continue to let yourself, your habits, people, sin, temptations, disobedience, doubt, unbelief, impatience, your flesh or weaknesses, keep you out of the Will, away from your blessings, and the promises God has for you. Rise up and conquer! You already have the tools within you to survive and to overcome, you just need to choose to use them. Every good and perfect gift comes from above, everything else is only temporary. Stop making excuses and start making changes! It's time to take the limits off and move up! Don't just be mediocre, know that you are the head and not the tail and walk in it! You are the one that God created to be the change! Yes! I'm talking about you! Be that change that others can see, not just when it is convenient for you or when it feels good but throughout the storms, in persecution, through suffering and even in pain. Stand up in your faith! I believe in you! I trust God for you! You will Win!

And David said to him, "Do not fear, for I will show you kindness for the sake of you father Johnathan, and I will restore to you all the land of Saul your father, and you shall eat at my table always. II Samuel 9:7.

David blessed Mephibosheth and Ziba because of the overflow and covenant made to Saul and Johnathan. You better see this thing for what it is! Some of us are just simply living in the overflow of those we are connected to. This is why it is important to stay connected to the Saints because your inheritance is among those who are sanctified. Why do you think the devil tries to convince you to stay away from those who have power, those that can influence you to change, those who are true ambassadors of Christ? He will have you hiding like Adam in the garden of Eden, it's a trap to keep you bound, keep you making excuses, and to keep you in sin. Come out from among them and LIVE! Don't you notice when you are not living right and are away from the fire things start gradually being stripped from you? Everything you have been blessed with starts crumbling little by little? It's a snare. That devil will use your weakest area to tempt you to come back to him, but you are the one that holds the ultimate decision. He will only dangle it in your face and make you believe this time it will be different or that you will just do it one more time and before you know it you are fully operating in it and have separated yourself. You start missing one service, then two, then a month and then it goes on and on until you find yourself totally under his control and you feel that it is hard to come out. You begin to feel that everyone that has power is against you and everyone that loves you is against you, NO, it's the trick of the enemy, RUN FOR YOU LIFE! He is a liar, a manipulator, a deceiver, run into Jesus, run into the house and get this Word, run for your life! You have the power to do so.

Prayer: Father God, I ask that you forgive me for taken those that you have placed around me for granted. Help me to see the devil for who he is by obtaining a closer relationship with you. You said in your Word if I draw nigh unto to you, you will draw nigh unto me. I ask right now that I learn to bind the devil on every side with the power that you have given unto me. In Jesus name. Amen

NOTES

WORDS OF ENCOURAGEMENT

Stop just existing and LIVE! Don't let your praise be just a feeling, let it be a decision. Look at yourself in the mirror and say: "I WILL LIVE ABOVE"! throughout the day whisper, I will live above: poverty, weaknesses, sin, what the enemy says, what the enemy tempt me with, sickness, defeat, depression, loneliness, oppression, lies, frustration, anger, unforgiveness, lust, envy, jealousy, insecurities, unresolved issues, and whatever else I deal with. I WILL LIVE ABOVE! Psalm 150:6 says, "Let everything that hath breath praise the Lord."

When you are up- Praise Him!

When you are down- Praise Him!

When you don't understand- Praise Him!

When you feel lonely- Praise Him!

When you are sick- Praise Him!

When you are without- Praise Him!

Change those tests into testimonies and your mess into messages while you praise him and watch God turn things around for you! Be encouraged, God is not through with you yet! When you are down to nothing, he is always up to something!

Inspired by Mother Doris Taylor

Having therefore these promises, dearly beloved, let us cleanse ourselves from all filthiness of the flesh and spirit, perfecting holiness in the fear of God. II Corinthians 7:1.

Be watchful and remain focused and prayerful, your adversary the devil is seeking whom he may devour. Be wise with your decision making knowing that every decision that you make at this point should reflect who you truly serve. You can't play with the devil and thing that you can just repent later of get it right tomorrow, or even wait until it doesn't work to try and get it right. Turn away now! Decide NOW! Heed the warning and LIVE! Your way will never work without God. Cleanse yourself from all iniquities and sin by repenting and submitting yourself to God. Allow him to clean you up, be honest with him because he already knows what you are dealing with. It is through him that you will have your deliverance. Victory will be the place where your breaking point becomes your turning point.

Prayer: Give me a true heart of repentance Lord so that I will be able to stand in these evil days. Help me to turn from my evil ways, serve and love you with all of my heart, soul, mind and strength. Fill me with your spirit that will teach me all things and help me to live a holy and righteous life. Sanctify me for your use in Jesus name. May I do the work of you who have sent me while it is day. Amen!

Inspired by Catrina Gooden

NOTES

WORDS OF ENCOURAGEMENT

Thus, saith the Lord unto you: "Arise! Go forth toward the promise and purpose I have already called you to. Everywhere your feet shall tread shall be blessed and I will give you the desires of your heart only if you be obedient to my Word. Be strong and courageous and do not fear for I am with you and I will never leave you nor forsake you. No man or devil will be able to stand against you all the days of your life. Continue to meditate on my Word both day and night and do all that is written in it and your way shall be made prosperous wherever you may go, and you will always have good success!" Psalm 23:6 says, "Surely goodness and mercy shall follow me all the days of my life: and I will dwell in the house of the Lord forever." The Lord is changing your story, go ahead and thank him in advance. It's already done! Claim it, receive it and believe it! You may stumble, yet you are still worthy of his love so don't stay down! Arise, keep holding on and striving for greatness! You must endure and hold on to your faith! You got this! Go and change the world!

Inspired by PeTrecia Ray

Let us hold fast to the confession of our Faith without wavering, for He is faithful that has promised. Hebrews 10:23

If you can just truly trust God with all of your heart and mind, things would be much easier for you. Get yourself out of the way and the struggle won't be as hard. The suffering will become easier knowing that he is working all things out for your good. It is not over until God says it's over, and it is not done until God says it's done. Your current situation is not the last plan God has for you. Pick yourself up, shake yourself and get back in your place! There is more stored up just for you but you must trust him at his Word and be patient enough to wait. Shout out:

This is not it for me!

I will come out!

What the devil means for my bad, God will turn it around for my good!

I just need to walk in my deliverance!

Walk in truth!

Walk in righteousness!

Walk in holiness!

Separate myself and believe!

I will not give up nor give in!

Take this week by force and conquer God's Will for your life!

Prayer: Take a moment to reflect on what God has already done for you in prayer and thank him for the promises yet on the way!

Inspired by Dyesha Shaku

NOTES

As Queens we will always turn pain into Power!

Life has knocked us down a few times.

 It showed us things we never thought we would see.

We experienced sadness and failures, but one thing for sure, we always got up!

We won't be distracted by comparison because we are captivated with purpose.

 We have learned to love, forgive, walk away, let go, try again, and persevere knowing that if it challenges us it will change us!

 We are clothed in strength and dignity and we laugh without fear of the future!

God is in us and we will not fail.

We are so strong but gentle,

 educated but humble,

fierce but compassionate,

so passionate yet rational,

and so disciplined, yet Free!

We always RISE,

We always CONQUER,

We always OVERCOME,

And we will always WIN!

How many others will be inspired by your story? Take these next pages to write down your testimony and share this book with someone else to encourage them along the way!

Your testimony:

Your testimony:

Your testimony:

Your testimony:

Your testimony:

Your testimony:

Your testimony:

Your testimony:

Your testimony:

Your testimony:

Your testimony:

Your testimony:

Your testimony:

Your testimony:

Your testimony:

Your testimony:

Your testimony:

Your testimony:

Your testimony:

Your testimony:

Your testimony:

Your testimony:

Your testimony:

And they overcame him by the blood of the Lamb, and by the word of their testimony! Revelation 12:11a

Made in the USA
Monee, IL
26 September 2020